As the Crow Flies

A FIRST BOOK OF MAPS

by Gail Hartman

illustrated by Harvey Stevenson

Aladdin Paperbacks

First Aladdin Paperbacks edition 1993
Text copyright © 1991 by Gail Hartman
Illustrations copyright © 1991 by Harvey Stevenson

Aladdin Paperbacks
An imprint of Simon & Schuster Children's Publishing Division
1230 Avenue of the Americas
New York, NY 10020

Manufactured in China
25 26 27 28 29 30

The text of this book is set in Souvenir Light.
The illustrations are rendered in pen and ink and watercolor.
Typography by Julie Quan and Christy Hale.

ISBN 978-0-689-71762-8
Library of Congress Catalog
Card Number: 93-22101

0413 SCP

For my mom
— G.H.

For Rose
— H.S.

AS THE EAGLE SOARS

From the mountains, a stream flows

through a meadow

where a tall tree
stands.

mountains

stream

tree

meadow

THE EAGLE'S MAP

A path winds around a farmhouse,

past a shed,

to a garden where the sweet greens grow.

garden

shed

farmhouse

my house

THE RABBIT'S MAP

AS THE CROW FLIES

A road runs through fields,

past the factory,

to city streets lined with houses.

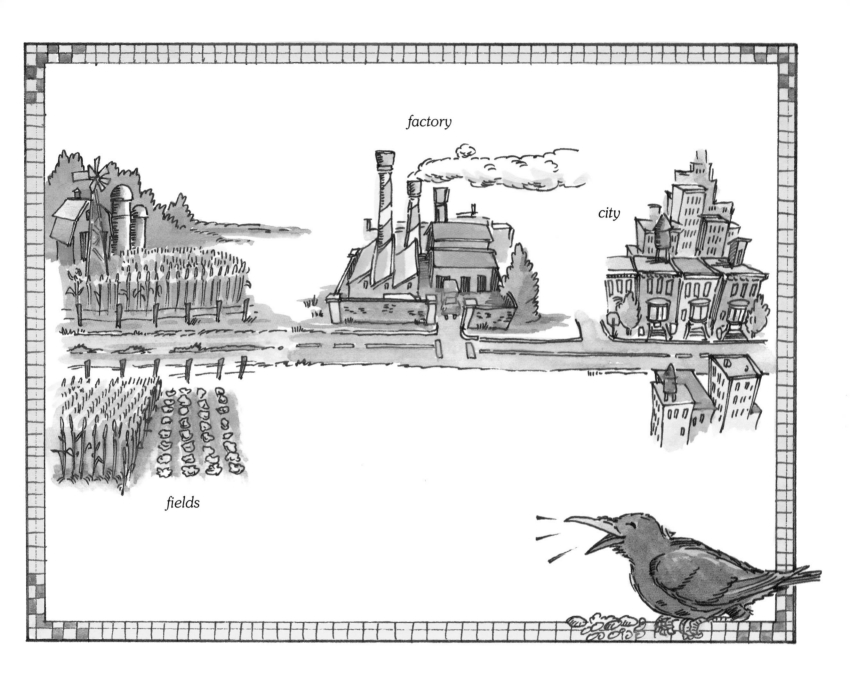

factory

city

fields

THE CROW'S MAP

15

AS THE HORSE TROTS

In the city, past the hot dog stand

and skyscrapers,

there is a park where music and the
sounds of children playing fill the air.

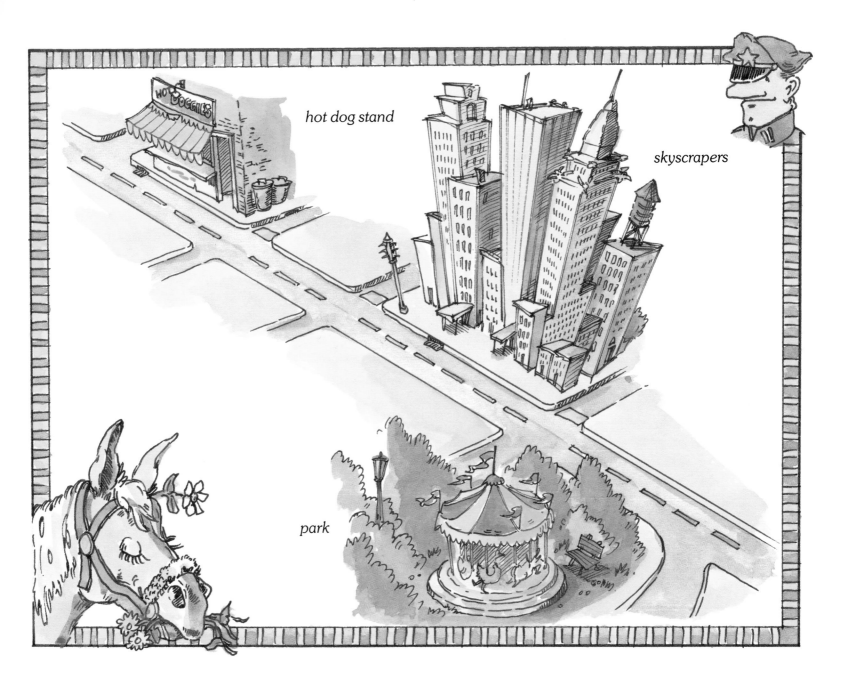

hot dog stand

skyscrapers

park

THE HORSE'S MAP

AS THE GULL GLIDES

Beyond the fishing boats in the harbor,

near the red brick lighthouse,

the ocean laps the shores of an island.

lighthouse

ocean

harbor

island

THE GULL'S MAP

When the moon shines, it shines on
the shores of the island in the ocean.

It shines on the park

and the houses in the city.

It shines on the garden near
the farmhouse in the country

and on the tree in the meadow,

near mountains that touch the sky.

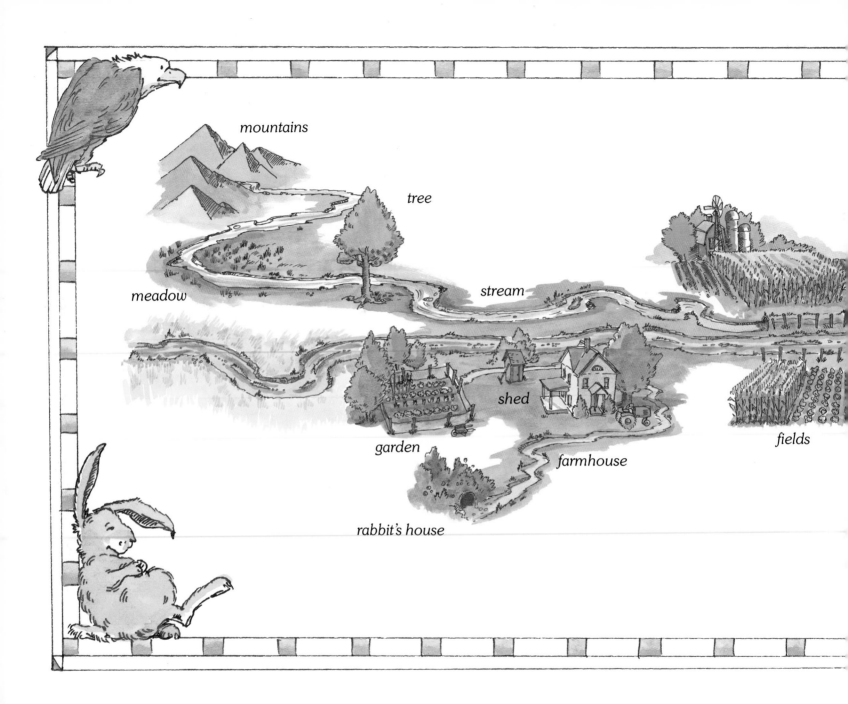

mountains

tree

meadow

stream

shed

garden

farmhouse

fields

rabbit's house

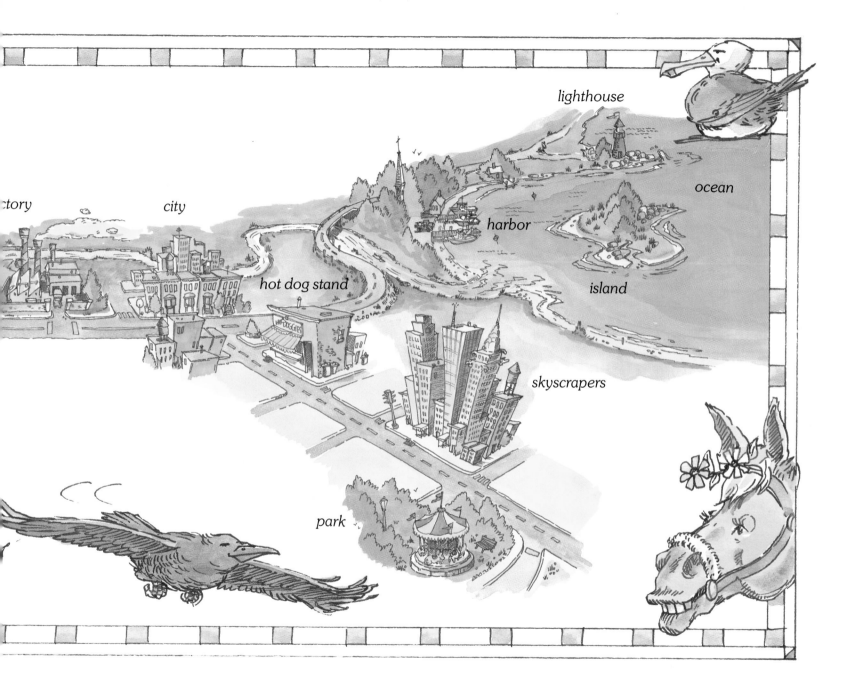

lighthouse

ocean

factory

city

harbor

island

hot dog stand

skyscrapers

park

THE BIG MAP